The Day the Ants Got Really Mad

by G.E. Stanley
illustrated by Sal Murdocca

Aladdin Paperbacks

To EEK,
who unleashed the madness,
and, as always,
to Gwen, James, and Charles

First Aladdin Paperbacks edition April 1996
Text copyright © 1996 by George Edward Stanley
Illustrations copyright © 1996 by Sal Murdocca

Aladdin Paperbacks
An imprint of Simon & Schuster
Children's Publishing Division
1230 Avenue of the Americas
New York, NY 10020

Designed by Randall Sauchuck and Chani Yammer
The text of this book is set in Garth Graphic.

Printed and bound in the United States of America

10 9 8 7 6 5 4

Library of Congress Cataloging-in-Publication Data
Stanley, George Edward.
The day the ants got really mad / by G.E. Stanley ; illustrated by Sal Murdocca. — 1st
Aladdin Paperbacks ed.
p. cm. — (Scaredy cats ; #1)
Summary: When Michael's family moves into a new house built on top of a gigantic anthill, the ants are not happy about it and are out for revenge.
ISBN 0-689-80858-5
[1. Ants—Fiction. 2. Moving, Household—Fiction.] I. Murdocca, Sal, ill. II. Title.
III. Series: Stanley, George Edward. Scaredy cats ; #1.
PZ7.S78694Day 1996
[Fic]—dc20 95-46716

Chapter One

"I wish you weren't moving," Jason Forest said. "I wish you were staying in your old house."

"I don't. Now I'll have my own room," Michael Trotter said. "You can spend the night with me."

They were sitting on the playground near the new swings.

They didn't feel like playing football.

It was too hot.

"But I can't ride my bike to your new house," Jason said. "It's too far away."

Michael would miss riding his bike to Jason's house, too.

But he wouldn't miss sleeping in the same room as his baby brother, Norton.

"I know," Michael said.

"Hey! Look at those red ants over there!" Jason said. "I've never seen so many red ants in my whole life!"

Michael looked. "There must be millions of them. I wonder what they're . . . ouch! Ouch!"

"What's wrong?" Jason asked.

"Something bit me!" Michael cried.

He stood up.

He looked around the playground.

He saw Mrs. Grayson, the playground monitor.

Michael ran to her.

"Something bit me on the leg. It really hurts."

"Then we'd better go see Nurse Hogan," Mrs. Grayson said.

She headed toward the front door of the school.

Michael was right behind her.

🐜 3 🐜

Then he stopped. "Ouch! Ouch!" he cried. "It bit me again!"

Mrs. Grayson hurried back to where Michael was hopping around.

"I think I know what it is. I remember where you were sitting. There are red ants all around that place."

Michael pulled up one leg of his jeans.

Two red ants were crawling on his knee.

"Oh! Oh! They're stinging me to death!"

Mrs. Grayson flicked the ants off with her finger. "Come on! Let's hurry!"

They ran toward the door.

Michael had never been stung by an ant before.

It really hurt.

"I think they're crawling all over me," he said.

"You're probably just imagining it," Mrs. Grayson said. "That happens."

Michael knew he wasn't imagining it.
He could feel them.

There were thousands of them.

They were all going to sting him, too. Any minute.

He wanted to cry. He wouldn't, though. You didn't cry in the third grade.

Finally, they reached Nurse Hogan's office.

Some other kid was lying on the cot. He had a thermometer in his mouth. He looked really sick.

But Michael wanted to tell him to get up.

Nobody was in more pain than he was.

"We have an ant-sting case here," Mrs. Grayson said. "On his leg."

Nurse Hogan looked at Michael. "That's the third one today. Were you sitting on the playground by the new swings?"

Michael nodded.

5

"Pull up your pants leg," Nurse Hogan said.

Michael did.

Nurse Hogan sprayed something cold where the ants had stung him.

It felt all tingly.

"That should stop the itching for a while," Nurse Hogan said.

"Thanks," Michael said. "It already feels better."

"That's good," Nurse Hogan said. "That's what we want."

"Why did they sting me?" Michael asked. "I wasn't bothering them."

"You probably made them mad," Nurse Hogan said. "You probably got in their way."

"How'd I do that?"

"Ants use their own trails to get to places. If you're sitting on one of them, they won't go around you. They'll go

6

over you. They may even go up your pants leg by mistake. When they realize they can't get out, they get scared. Then they get mad. That's why they sting you."

Michael couldn't believe he had caused the ants so much trouble. All he did was sit and talk to his best friend.

"We've got to do something about that anthill," Mrs. Grayson said. "It keeps getting bigger and bigger."

"I've never seen this many ants before," Nurse Hogan said. "It must be an invasion."

Michael closed his eyes.

He could see it now.

Millions and millions of ants invading his town.

They'd march down the streets.

They'd crawl all over the houses.

They'd go inside.

They'd crawl all over the people.

Michael opened his eyes.

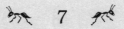

7

He was sweating.

He was breathing hard.

"Ouch! Ouch!" he cried. "They're all over me!"

Nurse Hogan looked at him.

Mrs. Grayson looked at him.

"Go get undressed," Nurse Hogan said. She opened the bathroom door. "Hurry up! There must be more ants inside your clothes."

Michael closed the door.

He took off his shirt.

He took off his shoes and socks.

He took off his jeans.

He took off his underwear.

Now he was standing naked in the bathroom. But he couldn't see any ants on his body.

There was a robe hanging on a hook on the door. He put it on.

"Ready?" Nurse Hogan said through the door.

"Ready," Michael said.

He opened the door. He handed Nurse Hogan his clothes. He closed the door.

He waited.

Finally, Nurse Hogan opened the door. "I got them all. There were three in your jeans. There were two in your shirt." She handed Michael his clothes. "Get dressed. You need to go on to class."

"Okay," Michael said.

He closed the door.

He looked at his clothes.

Suddenly, he didn't want to put them back on.

He was sure there were still ants in them. Some that Nurse Hogan had missed.

They were hiding.

They were probably really mad at him now.

They were just waiting to sting him.

Chapter Two

Michael decided to search his clothes himself.

He turned his shirt inside out.

He turned his jeans inside out.

He turned his underwear inside out.

He turned his socks inside out.

He took out his shoelaces. He opened up his basketball shoes as wide as he could.

He looked anywhere he thought an ant might be hiding.

He didn't find any more ants.

But he was sure they were there somewhere.

"Hurry, Michael! Get your clothes on," Nurse Hogan called. "You have to go to class."

Michael didn't want to get dressed.

He wanted to call his mother.

He wanted to ask her to bring him some new clothes. Some clothes that didn't have ants in them.

But Norton was sick. He was throwing up a lot. His mother wouldn't want to bring him to school.

What a pain baby brothers could be!

"Michael?"

"Yes?"

"Are you dressed?"

"Uh, almost," Michael said.

He looked at the inside of his clothes again.

He still didn't see anything.

He'd just have to take a chance.

Finally, he had everything turned right side out.

Then he had an idea.

If he put his clothes on slowly and

carefully, maybe he wouldn't disturb the ants.

Michael put on his underwear. Slowly. Carefully.

He put on his shirt. Slowly. Carefully.

He put on his jeans. Slowly. Carefully.

He put on his socks and shoes. Slowly. Carefully.

He stood perfectly still. So far, so good.

"Michael!" Nurse Hogan was getting mad. "Open that door!"

Michael opened the door. "I'm dressed," he said.

Nurse Hogan took a deep breath. "Go to your classroom," she said. She handed him a pass. She also handed him a note. "Give this to your parents. It tells them what I sprayed on your leg."

"Thank you for saving my life, Nurse Hogan," Michael said.

"You're welcome," Nurse Hogan said.

"And remember. If you don't make an ant mad, it won't sting you."

"I'll remember," Michael said.

He walked down the hallway. Slowly. Carefully.

Finally, he arrived at his classroom.

He stood at the door.

Mrs. Baylor looked at him.

The rest of the class looked at him.

"Are you all right?" Mrs. Baylor asked.

Michael nodded his head. Slowly. Carefully.

He handed Mrs. Baylor the pass from the nurse. Slowly. Carefully.

He walked to his seat. Slowly. Carefully.

He sat down. Slowly. Carefully.

"Are you sure?" Mrs. Baylor asked.

Michael nodded again. Slowly. Carefully.

"Well, I'm glad you made it back," Mrs. Baylor said. "We're going to see a movie for science. It's about ants."

"No!" Michael screamed.

Mrs. Baylor blinked. "Michael Trotter! What in the world is wrong with you?"

"Nothing! I'm sorry!" He couldn't tell anyone that his pants were full of ants. He'd never hear the end of it.

"Well, I certainly hope so," Mrs. Baylor said.

She pulled the blinds.

She turned on the VCR.

She turned off the light.

Michael began to feel funny.

Something was crawling down his leg.

He was sure it was a red ant.

Any minute it would sting him.

The music started.

The title of the movie came on. It was called: *Our Friend, the Ant.*

Michael couldn't believe it.

Whoever made this movie had never been stung by an ant.

The man in the movie talked about how ants turn up the soil and let in air.

He talked about how ants eat harmful insects.

He talked about how ants even pollinate plants.

But he didn't talk about how ants sting nice kids like Michael Trotter.

The movie showed the inside of an ant colony. There were tunnels everywhere.

It showed how some ants collect food.

It showed how some ants take care of the babies.

It showed the builder ants, the cleaner ants, the worker ants, the hunter ants, and the soldier ants.

Finally, it showed the most important ant of all: the queen.

Michael wondered what kinds of ants were in his pants.

The movie showed thousands and thousands of ants all over the world.

There were ants in the jungles.

There were ants in the mountains.

There were ants in the deserts.

There were ants in the cities.

There were ants in all the little towns like the one where Michael lived.

The man in the movie said there were a quadrillion living ants on earth.

Michael had never heard that number before.

At last, the movie was over.

Michael raised his hand. Slowly. Carefully.

"Yes, Michael?" Mrs. Baylor said.

"How much is a quadrillion?" he asked.

Mrs. Baylor smiled. "It's a one with fifteen zeros after it." She wrote it on the chalkboard.

Michael gulped.

The rest of the class gulped.

"Is that a lot?" Emily Halliday asked.

Mrs. Baylor nodded. "There are more ants than almost any other insect on earth. They're everywhere."

Michael believed her. He closed his eyes. He saw them. Ants! Ants! Ants! They were crawling all over him.

He screamed.

Chapter Three

Michael handed two pieces of paper to his mother.

"What are these?" she asked.

"Notes from school."

"What kind of notes?"

"One is from Nurse Hogan. It's about the ants."

"What about them?"

"They stung me. A whole lot of them. Nurse Hogan sprayed some cold stuff on my leg."

His mother read the note. "Oh, goodness. Well, let me see."

Michael pulled up his pants leg. "It's starting to itch again."

"It's still a little red, too. I'll spray it

some more. We have the same medicine as Nurse Hogan. Okay?"

"Okay," Michael said.

"Who's the other note from?"

"It's from Mrs. Baylor. She wants to know why I screamed so much in class today."

"Well, why did you?"

"We saw a movie about ants. I was thinking about them. They were crawling all over me."

His mother hugged him. "Well, I'll call Mrs. Baylor. I'll talk to her. I'm sure she'll understand."

Then she sprayed his leg.

It stopped itching.

"You must have had a rough day today."

"I did. It was awful."

"Didn't you see the ants before you sat down?"

"No," Michael said. "But I know how to look for them now."

"How?"

"There's a little hill of dirt. It's called an anthill. I'm going to stay away from anthills from now on."

"That's a good idea."

Michael thought it was a good idea, too.

"Well, I have something to tell you that might make you feel better," his mother said. "We're spending the first night in our new house tonight."

"Really?" Michael cried.

"Really!" his mother replied.

Michael jumped up and down.

Then he stopped.

He waited.

Nothing happened.

Maybe Nurse Hogan got all the ants out of his clothes after all.

"You need to pack the rest of

your things," his mother said. "Norton's sleeping in our room, so you won't disturb him."

"All right," Michael said.

He knew the first thing he was going to pack, too.

He went to his room.

Michael took off his clothes. Slowly. Carefully.

He put them all in a box.

He got a pencil from a drawer.

He wrote

ANT CLOZ

on the top of the box. He would never wear these clothes again.

Then he started packing the rest of his things.

His father came home from work.

Michael told him all about the ants.

His father sprayed his leg again.

Finally, they were all ready to leave their old house.

Suddenly, Michael felt funny about leaving.

It would take awhile to get used to the new house, he knew.

It would be like living in a hotel at first.

They drove out of town.

They turned down a narrow road.

"Here's where you'll catch the school bus," his mother said.

That was the only thing Michael didn't like. At his old house, he could ride his bike to school.

They made another turn.

Michael could see the house.

It looked really big.

"Who's that on the porch?" his mother asked.

"It looks like the Colliers," his father said. "They're our nearest neighbors."

"I hope they won't stay long," his mother said. "I don't feel like having company."

"They have a son in the second grade, Michael," his father said.

Michael looked. The boy seemed familiar. He was sure he had seen him at school. But he didn't know the names of the second graders. He sighed. He wished this boy were Jason.

His father stopped the car.

Michael got out.

The boy came over to him. "What's your name?"

Michael told him.

"My name's Frank. Want to play?"

"I guess," Michael said.

They ran around to the back of the house.

"I live just down the road. You can see my house from here," Frank said.

"I've always lived in the country."

"This is my first time," Michael said.

"You'll like it. You can do a lot of things. Maybe you and I can do some things together."

"Okay," Michael said. But he wasn't really sure. Frank was in second grade. He wondered if the kids at school would think he was a baby if he played with Frank.

"I was wondering something," Frank said.

"What?"

"Why did they build your house on top of it?"

Michael looked at him. "On top of what?"

"On top of the ant colony."

Michael gulped. He felt sick. "What do you mean?"

"They built your house on top of a huge ant colony. I know. I used to come

over here all the time and watch them. There are probably a billion ants under there. Maybe even a quadrillion."

Michael was finding it hard to breathe. He knew what a quadrillion was. A one with fifteen zeros behind it.

"Whose room is this?" Frank asked. He was pointing to a window on the side of the house.

"It's mine," Michael said.

Frank shook his head. "Too bad. It's right over the opening. Where all those ants come in and out."

Chapter Four

"Mom! Can I change rooms with Norton?" Michael asked.

His mother looked at him. "Why? We decorated your room the way you wanted. It's the color you asked for. It's the wallpaper you picked out. Why would you want to change?"

Michael shrugged. "I just do." He didn't want to tell her about the ant colony under his room.

"Do you want to sleep in a room with baby animals on the wall?"

"I don't care," Michael said.

He did, really.

He could never have his friends over. They'd make fun of him for sure.

Did he want his friends to laugh at him?
Or did he want the ants to sting him?
He'd have to choose.

"My friends like baby animals."

"No, Michael, I think you should sleep in your own room. At least for tonight. If you still feel the same way in the morning, then we'll talk to your father about changing."

Michael took a deep breath.

He had to think up a way to get out of his room.

He didn't even want to spend one night in it.

He thought and thought.

Finally, he thought of something.

He'd *pretend* to sleep in his room.

He'd go to bed.

He'd wait until his parents went to bed.

Then he'd get up.

He'd take his blanket and his pillow.

He'd tiptoe to the living room.

He'd sleep on the couch.

He'd get up early the next morning.

He'd get back in his bed. No one would know the difference.

Michael relaxed. He had this all figured out.

His mother ordered pizza for supper.

"I didn't know you could do that," Michael said. "I thought you had to live in town."

"We're not that far from town, Michael. We're just about two miles. They'll deliver out here. I'll give them a good tip, though. They won't mind that."

The pizza tasted wonderful.

His parents weren't too hungry. Michael got some extra slices.

"Dad, why did they build our house on top of the ants?"

His father looked at him. "What do you mean?"

"Frank said they built our house on top

of an ant colony. He said it was the biggest one he'd ever seen. He said my room was right over where they go in and out."

His mother smiled. "So that's why you wanted to change rooms."

Michael shrugged. He pretended it wasn't the reason. It didn't matter now, anyway. He had his plan. He wouldn't be sleeping in his room.

"There's nothing to worry about, son. There's a crawl space under the house," his father said. "The ants can still get in and out. They won't bother you."

"But won't they be mad?"

"Why would they be mad?"

"Maybe they didn't want a house on their land. Maybe they liked it the way it was."

"Well, this really isn't their land. It belonged to Mr. Ashton," his father said. "Now it belongs to us. I'll tell the ants to leave if they bother you."

Michael wondered if his father could do that.

He went to bed wondering.

But he didn't go to sleep.

He waited until he heard his parents go to bed.

Then he got up.

He picked up his pillow and blanket.

He tiptoed out of his room.

He went through two other rooms until he reached the living room.

He made up his bed on the couch.

He lay down and went to sleep.

He woke up with a start.

Something was strange.

He looked around.

He was back in his bedroom.

Something was crawling all over him.

He jumped out of bed.

He turned on the light.

His pajamas were covered with ants!

Chapter Five

Michael jumped up and down. "Mom! Dad!" he screamed.

He ran out of his room.

He ran down the hall.

He burst in to his parents' bedroom. "Mom! Dad!"

He turned on the light.

His father jumped up. "Michael, what in the world is wrong with you?"

"Ants! Ants! They're crawling all over me!"

His father looked at him. "I don't see any ants."

"You were probably just dreaming, dear," his mother said sleepily.

Michael looked down at his pajamas.

"They were there! I know they were. I woke up. They were crawling all over me. They must have fallen off."

"You're still just upset because of what happened at school this afternoon," his father said.

Michael sighed. Why didn't they believe him?

"Is that why you were sleeping in the living room?" his mother asked.

Michael nodded.

"You scared us," his mother said. "I couldn't go to sleep. I got up. I went in to check on you. You weren't in your room."

"We looked all over for you. That's when we found you in the living room," his father said. "I put you back in your own bed. I didn't see any ants."

"You don't believe me," Michael said. "You don't believe the ants were crawling all over me."

"We believe you think they were," his father said. "That's what we believe."

Michael knew he had been covered with ants. They were all over his pajamas. But they must have fallen off. When he jumped up and down.

But why hadn't they bitten him?

Suddenly, Michael remembered something Nurse Hogan had said. Ants only bite you if they're mad at you.

The ants were mad. But they weren't mad at *him*.

He'd be mad, too, if somebody built a house on top of his house.

Ants were smart, though. They knew it wasn't Michael's fault.

But they'd probably sting whoever built this house.

Michael relaxed.

"All right. I'll go back to my room now," he said. "I'll sleep in my own bed."

His mother stood up. "I'll lie down with you for a few minutes."

"No!" Michael said. It came out stronger than he meant. "I mean, it's okay. You don't have to. I feel better now."

He didn't want to take a chance.

The ants might be mad at his mother.

They might be mad at his father, too.

After all, they were the ones who paid the man to build the house.

"Good-night," Michael said.

He went back to his room and changed out of his pajamas. But he didn't get in bed.

He went to his bookshelf.

He took out a big book.

It was about insects. He had forgotten about it until just now.

His grandparents had given it to him for his birthday.

He had been disappointed.

He had hoped it was a toy.

He'd said thank you.

But he hadn't meant it.

Now he was glad.

He opened the book to the part about ants.

He wanted to find out what would happen if you built your house on top of an ant colony.

He started reading.

He couldn't believe it.

That man in the movie should have read this. These ants didn't sound friendly at all.

They fought wars.

They kidnapped children of other ants.

They ate birds.

They even ate small animals that got in their way.

Michael gulped. He wondered if the ants would consider him a small animal.

They were very strong.

They could lift things many times their own weight.

Finally, he saw it! It was at the top of the page. *Sometimes ants even live in houses!*

Is that what would happen to his new house? Would the ants decide to move in?

Michael closed the book.

He wished his family still lived in their old house. There weren't any ants in it.

Maybe it wasn't too late to move back.

He'd tell his parents in the morning that he wanted to move back to their old house.

He'd even sleep in the same room with Norton.

Michael took a deep breath.

He had suddenly thought of something.

When his parents had told him they were going to build a new house, Michael had said it was a great idea.

Maybe the ants knew he had said that, too.

They were probably really mad at *him*.

What was he going to do?

He yawned.

He was so sleepy.

He didn't want to think about this anymore.

He'd just close his eyes for a minute.

But he wouldn't go to sleep.

No way!

"Michael!"

Michael opened his eyes.

His mother was standing at his door.

She was screaming about something.

Then he felt them. The ants!

They were crawling all over him.

Chapter Six

"It's a miracle they didn't sting you, son," his father said.

"I guess they're not mad at me, after all, Dad," Michael said.

His father looked puzzled.

"We should have listened to you last night," his mother said. "We shouldn't have sent you back to your room without checking first."

"Well, we'll get rid of them today," his father said. "I'll call the bug man right now." He looked at his watch. "Oh. Oh. I'm late. I have to go to work now. Could you do it for me?"

"Yes," his mother said.

"I have a great idea," Michael said.

"Why don't we move back to our old house?"

"We're not going to move, Michael," his father said. "The ants are!"

"But the ants were here first, Dad," Michael said. "We shouldn't make them move."

"Michael," his father said, "we bought this house. It's ours. We're not moving."

Michael sighed.

He decided not to tell his parents that the ants would never move.

He knew a lot about ants now. Probably more than anyone else in the whole world.

They could get really mad.

He didn't want them mad at him again.

He didn't want them mad at his parents, either.

His father left for work.

His mother fixed breakfast for him and Norton.

Then Michael went outside.

He sat on the front porch steps.

He was bored. He wished he could play with Jason.

Then he remembered something his father had said.

There was a crawl space under the house.

A crawl space meant a space where you could crawl, didn't it?

So there had to be a door to it.

When he had walked around the house with Frank, he hadn't seen a door.

Maybe he hadn't seen it because it was *closed*!

And if it was closed, that meant maybe the ants couldn't get out.

And if they couldn't get out through the crawl space, they'd get out through his room!

What good did it do to have a crawl space if the ants couldn't use it?

He'd solve this problem.

He'd open the door!

He walked around the house.

Finally he found it.

It was just a little door.

But it was big enough for the ants.

Michael looked at it. It was big enough for him, too.

He'd like to see what that anthill looked like.

The ants wouldn't mind if he looked.

They'd know he was the one who had opened the door for them.

They'd be happy.

Now they wouldn't have to live in his house.

They could get out.

They could go anywhere they wanted to.

Michael opened the door.

He peeked inside. He couldn't see anything.

It was dark. He needed a flashlight.

He went back inside the house.

He borrowed the flashlight his father kept by the side of his bed.

He went back outside.

He shined the flashlight under the house.

He saw the anthill at once.

But it wasn't a hill.

It was a *mountain*.

It went almost to the top of the crawl space.

Michael wanted to get closer.

He couldn't believe how huge this ant mountain was.

He got down on his knees.

He shined the flashlight ahead of him.

It gave off a lot of light.

Now it wouldn't be scary at all.

He crawled in a few more inches.

He was halfway into the opening.

He took a deep breath.

He crawled in some more.

Now he was all the way under the house.

It wasn't so bad.

He'd also have something to tell Mrs. Baylor when she talked about ants.

He'd talk about the biggest ant *mountain* in the world.

They might even take a field trip out to his house. So they could see his friends, the ants.

He'd take turns showing everyone in the class the ant mountain.

He wouldn't be afraid anymore.

He crawled closer and closer to the ant mountain.

He could see ants crawling all over it.

There were hundreds. There were

thousands. There were millions.

There might even be a quadrillion.

He could see that number on the chalkboard now. A one with fifteen zeros after it.

This was probably the front door for all the ants in the world.

Maybe all those other anthills were just back doors.

Then the crawl space door slammed shut.

The wind must have blown it closed, Michael thought.

He started breathing fast.

He couldn't turn around. He had to back up.

He backed up as fast as he could.

He reached the crawl space door.

He tried to open it. But he couldn't.

He was trapped under his house with all the ants in the world!

Chapter Seven

Michael kicked at the door.

"Mom! Mom!" he cried. "Help me!"

He shined the flashlight at the ant mountain.

He was sure the ants were getting irritated.

They probably didn't like loud noises.

He couldn't help it, though.

He had to scream.

"Mom! Mom! I'm under the house! Get me out!"

He kicked at the door some more. It wouldn't budge.

He shined his flashlight at the ant mountain again.

He couldn't believe what he saw.

The ants were marching toward him!
They must be soldiers, he thought.
They fought wars.
They kidnapped little children.
He had to get out of there!
He tried to turn around.
He couldn't.
He dropped the flashlight. It went out.
"Mom! Mom!" he cried again.
Suddenly, the door opened.
The crawl space flooded with light.
"Michael? Is that you?"
His mother had heard him!

"Yes! Yes! It's me!" He backed out of the crawl space as fast as he could.

"What in the world were you doing under the house?"

"Quick, Mom! Shut the door. They're coming to get me!"

His mother shut the door. "Who's coming to get you?"

"The ants. A quadrillion of them. That's a one with fifteen zeros!"

His mother just looked at him.

"The anthill! It's not a hill, Mom! It's a mountain! It really is!"

His mother didn't say anything. She just looked sad. She was probably sad because she had a weirdo for a son.

He shouldn't have gone under the house.

Why did he think the ants would like his stupid idea? They didn't want to go out through the crawl space door. They wanted to take over his room!

"Let's go back into the house," his mother finally said.

"Okay," Michael said.

But he didn't go to his room.

He went to the living room to watch television.

It was snowy.

They didn't have cable in the country.

His father said they'd have it in a couple of months.

That didn't do any good now, though.

All the channels were snowy.

Outside, a horn honked.

Michael ran to the door.

It was the bug man.

"He's here, Mom!" he called.

His mother came to the door. "It's under the house. There's a crawl space. Ants. Lots of them. They're coming inside my son's room."

"They're crawling all over me," Michael added.

The bug man blinked in surprise.

"Show him where the door to the crawl space is, Michael," his mother said. "I need to take care of Norton."

Michael led the bug man to the crawl

space. "It's not an anthill," he said. "It's an ant *mountain*."

"That's okay. This stuff will take care of them," the bug man said. "They'll be gone in a couple of hours."

The bug man crawled under the house.

Michael sat by the door and waited. He didn't want the same thing to happen to the bug man that had happened to him.

He wondered if the bug man would scream when he saw the ants.

He waited.

But the bug man didn't scream.

Finally, the bug man backed out from under the house. "You're right. It is big. I had to give it a double dose. That'll take care of them, though."

The bug man left.

Michael went back into the house.

He played with Norton.

He watched snowy television.

His father came home.

They all had dinner.

They watched some more snowy television.

Then Michael went to bed. He was very tired. He could sleep tonight. He didn't have to worry about the ants.

During the night, he woke up.

His bed was moving.

Someone was carrying it through the door.

He looked down on the floor.

With the night-light, he could see them.

There were ants everywhere!

Chapter Eight

The ants were carrying his bed out of his room!

Michael knew they were strong.

He knew they could carry several times their own weight.

But this was ridiculous.

Now he was in the living room.

His mother kept a lamp on in there all night.

Michael stuck his head under the bed.

He counted ten ants under each foot.

There was also a column of ants marching along each side of the bed.

He started to call his parents.

Then he decided not to. He wanted to see what the ants planned to do.

Actually, this was kind of fun.

Unless the ants planned to take him outside. Then crawl all over him. Then sting him.

But why would they do that?

They could have done that in his room.

They must be planning something else.

Then Michael remembered the bug man.

He was supposed to get rid of the ants. It would only take a couple of hours, he had said.

But they were all still alive.

Maybe they hadn't eaten whatever the bug man had fed them. The ants were too smart for him.

They had reached the front door. The bed stopped.

The door opened.

When it was open all the way, the bed started to move again.

The ants carried the bed down the steps of the porch.

They carried it out into the front yard.

They dropped it with a thud.

Michael couldn't believe how dark it was in the country.

He could see the stars. He could see the moon.

But he couldn't see the ants on the ground.

He knew they were there, though.

He could hear them humming.

He had heard that noise before.

It was in a movie about giant ants.

The humming noise was the sound they made when they were really mad.

They were really mad now.

Michael wanted to put his foot down.

But he was afraid the ants would start crawling all over him.

So he kept his foot on the bed.

He waited.

He'd wait until it was light, he decided. Until he could see where the ants were on the ground.

Then he heard a noise.

It sounded like a door opening.

It was. It was the front door.

Another bed was coming through it.

It was his parents' bed.

He couldn't believe it.

The ants were moving his parents out, too.

He opened his mouth to call them.

Then he closed his mouth.

His parents were still asleep. He was sure of it. If they weren't, they would have said something.

If they woke up, they'd be upset.

They'd try to stop the ants.

The ants wouldn't let them.

They'd crawl all over his parents.

They'd sting them.

Michael kept his mouth closed.

The ants moved his parents' bed next to his.

They dropped it with a thud.

But his parents never woke up.

The ants kept moving the furniture out of the house.

They moved Norton's crib.

They moved the living room furniture.

They moved the dining room furniture.

They moved the stove. They moved the refrigerator.

By dawn, Michael was sure they had moved everything out of the house.

"Now it belongs to the ants," he murmured.

Finally, it got light.

His parents woke up. The sun was in their eyes.

"What in the world!" his father said.

His mother screamed.

His father looked over at him. "What's going on here, Michael?"

"The ants did it," Michael said. "The ants moved us out of the house!"

His father stood up. "They did *what*?"

"Michael!" his mother cried. "How could a bunch of little ants do something like this?"

"They're very strong," Michael said.

His father ran toward the house.

Michael followed him.

His father opened the door. He looked inside. "Oh, no!" he cried.

Michael looked, too.

The ants were everywhere.

They covered the floor.

They covered the walls.

They covered the ceiling.

Chapter Nine

Michael's father found his car keys.

They were on top of the dresser. Where they always were.

They hadn't fallen off when the ants moved the dresser outside.

"They're very good movers," his mother said. "They're better than some humans I know."

"I'm in no mood for jokes," his father said. "I'm going to town. I'm going to get the bug man. We're going to get rid of these ants today." He looked at Michael. "You're going with me."

Michael knew everyone blamed him.

They thought the ants were all his fault.

But they weren't.

His father started toward the car.

"You'd better get dressed, George," his mother called.

His father came back.

He stood behind the dresser.

He put on some clothes.

Michael decided to keep his pajamas on.

People didn't care what kids wore.

He didn't want to change outside in front of everyone.

They got into the car and drove into town.

There were hardly any cars on the street.

"I forgot it was Sunday," his father said. "I probably won't be able to get the bug man to do anything."

He was right.

The bug man was still in bed. "I don't

get rid of bugs on Sundays. And Monday's a holiday. So you'll have to wait until Tuesday."

Michael looked at his father.

He could tell he was really mad.

But his father didn't say anything.

They drove back to their house in silence.

His mother had breakfast ready. "It's what was in the refrigerator," she said.

They sat down at the table.

They had fruit. They had cereal and milk. The milk was warm.

"What are we going to do?" his mother asked his father. "We can't stay here all day."

"We can and we will," his father said. "No ants are going to force me off my property."

His father was wrong. Michael wanted to say so. He wanted to tell his father how much he knew about ants. But he didn't think this was the right time.

They lived outside all day.

Some new neighbors came by to visit. Michael's father was in a really bad mood. The people didn't stay very long.

Finally, it was time to go to bed.

"It's like camping out," his mother said. "Look at those stars."

His father just grunted.

It really was like camping out, Michael thought.

He pulled the sheet up around him.

He looked up at the stars.

There were hundreds. There were thousands. There were millions.

He wondered if there were a quadrillion. A one with fifteen zeros after it.

He wondered if there were more stars than ants.

Finally, he went to sleep.

He woke up.

He was on the ground.

No! He wasn't on the ground. He was *almost* on the ground. He was moving. Someone was carrying him.

The ants!

The ants were carrying him somewhere!

But where?

His head went inside the crawl space under his house.

It was hard to breathe.

He tried to struggle free. But the ants held him tight. He couldn't get away.

Suddenly, a light went on. Where was it coming from? he wondered.

Then Michael saw a flashlight. It was the flashlight he had dropped when he was in the crawl space. He had forgotten about it.

The ants carried him up the ant mountain.

They carried him down inside it.

They're taking me inside the ant colony! he realized.

Down and down they went.

But the light from the flashlight penetrated even here. Michael could see all the different chambers.

He saw a hunter bringing in a caterpillar for food.

He saw the cleaners dumping garbage in the garbage chamber.

He saw the granary where the ants stored their grain.

He saw them milking honeydew from aphids.

He saw a worker carrying baby ants to the nursery.

He saw all kinds of wonderful things.

This is why they brought me here! Michael suddenly realized. *They want me to understand what's going on. They want me to see how important it is.*

"I understand!" Michael said. "I'll try to help you."

The ants carried him out of the chambers.

They reached the entrance.

They carried him up and down the mountain.

They carried him through the crawl space and out the door.

They put him back in his bed.

Michael felt really strange.

But he wasn't afraid anymore.

He had another idea. This was his best idea.

In the morning, he'd tell his father.

He only hoped he could convince him they didn't need the bug man anymore.

Chapter Ten

Michael opened his eyes.

His mother was rocking Norton.

His father was sitting on the side of their bed.

"I think we should have stayed in a motel last night," his mother said. "The house is so overrun with ants that I can't even go inside to take a bath. I feel terrible."

"I'm sorry you feel terrible, but I will not let those ants get away with this," his father said. "This is the house I've always wanted. I'll never leave it!"

Michael sat up. "Dad? I have a new idea."

His father shook his head. "I don't

want to hear a new idea, Michael. I want to get rid of those ants."

"Listen to what he has to say, dear," his mother said.

"All right," his father said. "What's your new idea?"

Michael took a deep breath. "Why don't we just move our house to town?"

"Maybe that's not a bad idea," his mother said.

His father looked at them. "Do you have any idea how much it costs to move a house?" he yelled. "I'll never give in to those ants!"

His mother sighed.

Michael sighed, too.

Norton burped.

Michael knew the ants would never leave their house.

He knew his father would never leave it, either.

Would they have to live outside for-
ever? he wondered.

What if it rained?

What if it snowed?

All day long, they just sat around and
listened to the ants.

They could hear them inside their
house. They were making humming
sounds.

Michael knew they were still mad.

He knew they'd stay mad, too.

Finally, it got dark.

Everyone went to bed.

During the night, Michael woke up.

His bed was moving.

What was going on? he wondered.

Then he knew.

But he couldn't believe it.

The ants were moving him and his
furniture back into the house.

When everything was finally in
place, the ants all left his room.

Michael got out of bed.

He looked out the window.

The ants were moving the rest of the furniture back into the house, too.

Had they given up after all? he wondered.

He couldn't believe it.

Finally, all was quiet.

Michael was disappointed.

He didn't want to live out in the country.

But now he was sure he'd have to.

His father had won the battle.

He had beaten the ants.

And he'd probably want to stay here to make sure they never came back.

Michael closed his eyes.

He was very tired.

᛭   ᛭   ᛭

The sun awakened him.

That's funny! he thought.

He was positive that in the morning the sun was on the other side of his new house.

He sat up and looked around.

Everything seemed normal. Except the sun.

Michael got out of bed.

There were no ants around anywhere.

They were probably back in their colony. Underneath his room.

They were probably really upset because they had lost, too.

Michael wondered if they'd ever come back.

They might, he decided, if they got mad enough again.

He went to the window and looked out.

He couldn't believe what he saw.

There were houses across the street.

He ran to the front door and went outside.

Cars were driving by. Kids were riding bicycles. Some of them waved at him.

They were back in town!

How had it happened? he wondered.

Then he knew.

The ants!

They had moved the house into town!

They hadn't lost.

They had won!

Then Michael noticed a sign on the front lawn.

It read: LOT FOR SALE.

He laughed.

The ants even knew where there was a vacant lot for sale.

Michael ran back into his house.

"Mom! Dad!" he cried. "Wake up! I have a surprise for you!"